RICHVIEW

A
GIFT

A
GIFT

By Claudia Fregosi

Prentice-Hall, Inc., Englewood Cliffs, New Jersey

Printed in the United States of America •J

Prentice-Hall International, Inc., London
Prentice-Hall of Australia, Pty. Ltd., North
   Sydney
Prentice-Hall of Canada, Ltd., Toronto
Prentice-Hall of India Private Ltd., New Delhi
Prentice-Hall of Japan, Inc., Tokyo

Library of Congress Cat-
aloging in Publication
Data

Fregosi, Claudia.
  A gift.

  SUMMARY: Want-
ing to express his love
for his wife, a man fi-
nally finds a way to
combine into one gift all
of the things that she
loves most.
  [1. Gifts—Fiction]
  I. Title.
PZ7.F884Gi   [E]
  76-9015
ISBN 0-13-356220-4

To Bill
and
Stephania

Once upon a time there lived a man and a woman.

The man loved his wife very much. He wanted to show her how special his love for her was.

He decided to make her a pair of slippers.

"Dear wife," he said. "I will make you slippers of the softest leather."

The woman smiled. "There is no leather as soft as your kiss. Just give me a kiss."

But her husband wanted to make her a gift.
"I will make you a necklace strung with the
biggest beads."

"There are no beads bigger than your hug. I'd rather have a hug," said the wife.

The man really did want to make her a gift.
He thought hard.
"I will make you a bracelet cast with the
brightest silver."

"There is no silver brighter than your smile," said his wife. "I like it when you smile."

Her husband had made up his mind.
That night while she slept, he was think-
ing. Finally he said, "I will make my wife a
blanket soft as a kiss, big as a hug, and bold
as my brightest smile."

He began to spin and weave. He worked all
night long.
Even the dog picked some of his very best
whiskers and wove them into the blanket.

When the man and the dog decided it was a
blanket, it was finished.

His wife woke up and he gave her the blanket.
"It is made of plain wool, but whenever you use it, I will give you a kiss, a hug, and a smile," he said.

"It's lovely! I'll use it always!" said his wife.
And she did.